THE CASE
OF VAMPIRE
VIVIAN

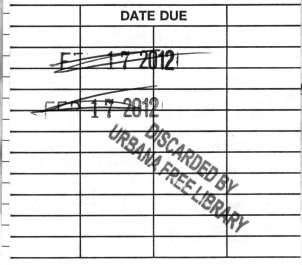

by Michelle Knudsen
illustrated by Amy Wummer

The Kane Press
New York

Acknowledgements: Our thanks to James G. Doherty, General Curator, The Bronx Zoo, New York City and Barbara French, Conservation Officer, Bat Conservation International, Austin, Texas for helping us make this book as accurate as possible.

Book Design/Art Direction: Edward Miller

Library of Congress Cataloging-in-Publication Data

Knudsen, Michelle.
 The case of Vampire Vivian / by Michelle Knudsen ; illustrated by Amy Wummer.— 1st U.S. ed.
      p. cm. — (Science solves it!)
 Summary: When Molly and her sister notice bats in their neighborhood for the first time, they become suspicious of the new girl in school nicknamed Vampire Vivian.
  ISBN 1-57565-127-0 (alk.paper)
 [1. Bats—Fiction. 2. Schools—Fiction. 3. Sisters—Fiction.] I. Wummer, Amy, ill. II. Title. III. Series.
PZ7.K7835 Cas 2003
[Fic]—dc21

                                                                2002156047

10 9 8 7 6 5 4 3 2

First published in the United States of America in 2003 by The Kane Press.
Printed in Hong Kong.

www.kanepress.com

There was a new girl in Molly's class—a
weird new girl. She had a thing about bats.

She had bat stickers all over her notebooks.
And she wore a bat T-shirt. She even had bat
earrings! It was creepy.

The new girl had moved in right down the
street from Molly. Her name was Vivian.

Molly told her parents about Vivian after
dinner. "The other kids call her Vampire
Vivian," she said. "She's kind of scary."

Molly's little sister, Lisa, dropped her dishtowel. "She's a *vampire*?" she asked in a small voice.

"That's just what they call her," Molly said. "Because of the bats."

"Vampires aren't real, sweetie," their mom told Lisa. Lisa still looked scared.

That night, Lisa jumped into Molly's bed. A bat had flown by her window. "It's her!" she gasped. "It's Vampire Vivian! She's trying to get me!"

In some made-up stories, vampires change into bats. Scary myths like this are one reason many people are afraid of bats.

Molly could barely see the bat flying away in the darkness. "Don't be silly," she said. "Vivian isn't *really* a vampire."

"Then where did the bat come from?" Lisa demanded.

"That's a good question," said Molly. "I've never seen a bat around here before."

On the way to school, Molly told her friends Louis and Frank about the bat.

"You don't think Vivian really could be a vampire, do you?" asked Louis.

"I guess we'll just have to find out," Molly said.

When Molly got to class, she made a list.
Then she looked it over.

What I Know
About Vampires:
1. can't go out in
daylight
2. sleep all day
3. drink blood
4. can turn into bats
5. hate garlic

Vivian had no trouble going out in daylight.
She was sitting right there at her desk. She was
wide awake, too.

Molly showed her list to Louis and Frank.
"Vivian drinks milk," said Frank. "And she
had garlic mashed potatoes at lunch."
"But what about the bat Molly saw?" asked
Louis. "How else do you explain it?"

That evening, Molly waited. Sure enough,
a bat flew by the window again. In fact, *three*
bats flew by.

"What are they doing out there?" Lisa
whispered from under her blanket.

"Just swooping around," Molly said.

Molly noticed more bats by the streetlight. But they weren't the only flying things. There was something else—something very small.

Bugs, she realized. The bats were chasing bugs!

How do bats see tiny insects in the dark? They use their ears! Bats send out high squeaks. The sounds bounce off objects and send echoes back to the bats' ears. From these echoes, bats can tell where something is, how big it is, and which way it's moving.

"Why would vampires chase bugs?" asked
Frank, when Molly told him what she'd seen.

"Maybe they're not very smart vampires,"
said Louis.

"Maybe they're just regular bats," Molly said.

"But why did they show up right after
Vivian moved in?" asked Frank.

"I wish I knew," said Molly. "We'd better find
out more about bats."

After school, they went to Frank's house to search the internet. There were *lots* of bat sites. "I guess Vivian's not the only person who has a thing about bats," Frank said.

If you want to find out more about bats, visit www.batcon.org or www.batroost.com.

Molly wrote down all the interesting facts they found. Frank printed out pictures. Louis kept everyone supplied with cookies and milk.

1. There are more than 1,000 kinds of bats!
2. Bats live all over the world.
3. Bats are the only flying mammal.
4. Bats are NOT blind!!!
5. Biggest bat is the giant flying fox—its wing span is 6 feet!!
6. Smallest bat is the bumblebee bat of Thailand. Its wing span is 6 inches.
7. Bats sleep in the daytime and wake up at night.

Molly watched the sky as she walked home. It wasn't dark enough for the bats to be out. The weird thing was she almost wanted to see them. Bats weren't nearly as scary as she had thought.

Many people are afraid of bats because they don't know much about them. Some people worry that bats will get tangled up in their hair, but that's unlikely. A bat that can find a tiny bug can easily avoid flying into something as big as a person!

At lunch the next day, Louis took out some
library books about bats. Molly set out her
notes, too.

Suddenly, a shadow fell across the table.
Molly looked up. Then she poked Frank and
Louis. They looked up, too.

It was Vampire Vivian.

"Hey," she said. "I didn't know you guys were interested in bats, too!"

Vivian was smiling. Somehow she seemed less weird.

"Uh . . ." Molly stammered. "We're trying to find out why there are suddenly all these bats around my house."

"I can explain that," Vivian said. "It's because of my bat house!"

Molly, Frank, and Louis stared at her.

"Your *what?*" Frank asked, finally.

"My bat house," said Vivian. "It's a little house my mom and I built to attract bats."

"You mean, you invited bats to come live near you?" asked Louis. "On purpose?"

Vivian laughed. "Why don't you come over after school and I'll show you?"

Molly nodded slowly. So did Frank and Louis. This was just too weird to pass up.

There are fewer and fewer bats in the world. One reason is that bat habitats are being destroyed. Bat houses give bats a safe place to live.

"I still don't get why people would want bats to live near them," said Louis on the way to Vivian's house.

"Because bats are so cool!" Vivian said.

Louis rolled his eyes. "I meant normal people," he muttered.

Vivian laughed. "Well for one thing, bats help get rid of pests like mosquitoes. Some bats can eat twelve hundred insects in one hour!"

"Wow," said Molly. Vivian sure knew a lot about bats.

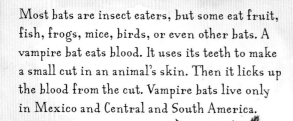

Most bats are insect eaters, but some eat fruit, fish, frogs, mice, birds, or even other bats. A vampire bat eats blood. It uses its teeth to make a small cut in an animal's skin. Then it licks up the blood from the cut. Vampire bats live only in Mexico and Central and South America.

The bat house was attached to the back of Vivian's house. "Are there bats in there right now?" asked Frank.

Vivian nodded. "A colony of big brown bats moved in last week," she said.

Vivian passed around binoculars so everyone could see the bats better. "They're hanging upside down. You can just see their furry little heads."

"There sure are a lot of them," Frank said.

Molly tried to count them, but the bats were squished too close together. It was hard to tell where one bat ended and another began. "I wish I could see a big brown bat close up," she said.

"I have a great picture of one right here in my bat album," said Vivian.

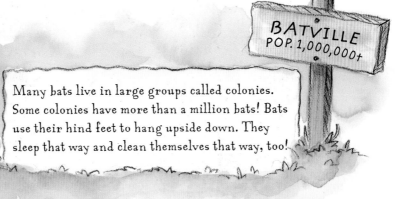

BATVILLE
POP. 1,000,000+

Many bats live in large groups called colonies. Some colonies have more than a million bats! Bats use their hind feet to hang upside down. They sleep that way and clean themselves that way, too!

"This *is* a great picture," Molly said.

"It makes me want to see some real live bats swooping around," said Louis.

"Me, too!" Frank said.

BAT ANATOMY

claw

second finger

thumb (first finger)

forearm

ears

third finger

fourth finger

fifth finger

leg

feet

tail

wing membrane (skin)

Remember. Never touch a bat! Like raccoons and other wild animals, bats may carry a dangerous disease called rabies.

"Just stay until sunset," Vivian said. "That's when the bats fly out of their house to hunt for food."

Vivian's mom thought that was a great idea. "Why don't you all stay for dinner, too?" she said.

Big brown bats can fly as fast as 15 miles an hour. How do bats change direction when they are flying? They move their long fingers and change the shape of their wings.

After dinner, they all watched as the bats
came streaming out into the night sky.
Even Louis had to admit that bats were
pretty cool.

A few days later, Vivian came to Molly's house for dinner. Vivian had been a really good sport about the whole vampire thing.

"I'm not worried about vampires anymore," Lisa told her. "Not since I met this new boy. I'm pretty sure he's a werewolf."

Vivian and Molly laughed. Forget bats and vampires. Little sisters were the weird ones.

THINK LIKE A SCIENTIST

Molly thinks like a scientist—and so can you!

Scientists ask questions and then look for answers.
One of the ways they find answers is by collecting and
organizing information. They collect information from
many different places—even from other scientists!

Look Back
Where do Molly and her friends go to collect information?
Look at pages 14 and 17. On page 22, Molly learns something new about bats. Where does this information come
from? On pages 24-25, Molly learns even more. How does
she get information this time?

Try This!
Collect 26 animal names, one for each letter of the
alphabet. Start by writing the letters from A to Z down
the side of a page. Then fill in as many names as you can.
If you get stuck you can look on the computer, in books
and magazines, or ask people to help!

To get you started, here is the name
of one animal: xenops (a bird).
Can you collect 25 more?